Gods of Legend

THOR

ERIC BRAUN

WORLD BOOK

BOLT

This World Book edition of *Thor*
is published by agreement between
Black Rabbit Books and World Book, Inc.
© 2018 Black Rabbit Books,
2140 Howard Dr. West,
North Mankato, MN 56003 U.S.A.
World Book, Inc.,
180 North LaSalle St., Suite 900,
Chicago, IL 60601 U.S.A.

Marysa Storm, editor; Michael Sellner, designer; Omay Ayres,
photo researcher

Library of Congress Control Number: 2016049945

ISBN: 978-0-7166-9313-0

Printed in the United States at CG Book Printers,
North Mankato, Minnesota, 56003. 3/17

CONTENTS

CHAPTER 1

An Ancient Story. 4

CHAPTER 2

Norse Mythology. 8

CHAPTER 3

God of the Sky
and Thunder. 18

CHAPTER 4

The Final Battle. 26

Other Resources. 30

An ANCIENT Story

The god Thor drove his **chariot** through the sky. Thunder cracked around him as he sped through the air. His red hair whipped in the wind. Up ahead, a great giant waited. Their **duel** was about to begin.

Thor threw his magical hammer. At the same time, the giant hurled a huge stone. The two weapons hit each other. The stone exploded into thousands of pieces.

Clash of Weapons

Pieces of stone flew all over the world. One piece stuck inside Thor's head. But the stone didn't stop his hammer. The weapon kept going. It struck the giant's head and killed him. Thor was hurt, but he won the battle.

Thor traveled in a chariot. Two large goats pulled it.

CHAPTER 2

Norse
MYTHOLOGY

The story of Thor is a Norse **myth**. **Ancient** people told stories to explain the world. Many myths were about gods. Norse people believed gods, such as Thor, lived among them.

Norse people lived in northern Europe from the 700s to about 1100. They spread their stories and beliefs when they traveled.

The Vikings were Norse warriors.

THOR IN THE WORLD OF THE ANCIENT NORSE

Norse people may have worn **charms** shaped like Thor's hammer. Such charms have been found in several countries.

ICELAND

DENMARK

NORWAY

SWEDEN

The Favorite God

Stories say Thor was the son of Odin. Odin ruled over all the gods. He was the father of all people. But many Norse people loved Thor the most. Stories say he kept people safe.

Thor was especially important to farmers. They believed he blessed their lands.

Protector

The ancient Norse also believed giants lived in their world. Giants were the enemy of gods and humans. Thor was a mighty warrior. He fought off the giants.

Norse stories say giants and gods have fought since the beginning of time. Odin and his brothers killed the very first giant. They made the earth from his body.

YGGDRASIL

The Norse believed the **universe** had three levels. The levels were part of a giant tree. The tree was called Yggdrasil (IG-druh-sil).

MIDDLE LEVEL
where humans and giants live

16

TOP LEVEL
where the gods live

RAINBOW BRIDGE
connects top level to middle level

LOWER LEVEL
the underworld

17

CHAPTER 3

God of the Sky and THUNDER

People believed Thor ruled the sky. He was the god of thunder. His chariot made thunder when he drove it. His hammer made lightning when he threw it. When it stormed, people thought it meant Thor was fighting.

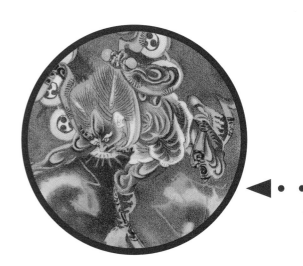

Gods
of Thunder

Many ancient beliefs have a god of thunder.

ZEUS
Greek mythology

RAIJIN
Japanese mythology

INDRA
Hindu mythology

Powerful Hammer

Thor fought with his mighty hammer. Stories say dwarfs made it. The hammer could never break. It returned to Thor's hand after he threw it. The hammer could even change size. It could become small enough to hide in Thor's shirt.

Thor wore a belt of strength and iron gloves. The belt made him stronger. The gloves helped him use the hammer.

LARGE BEARD

HAMMER

THOR

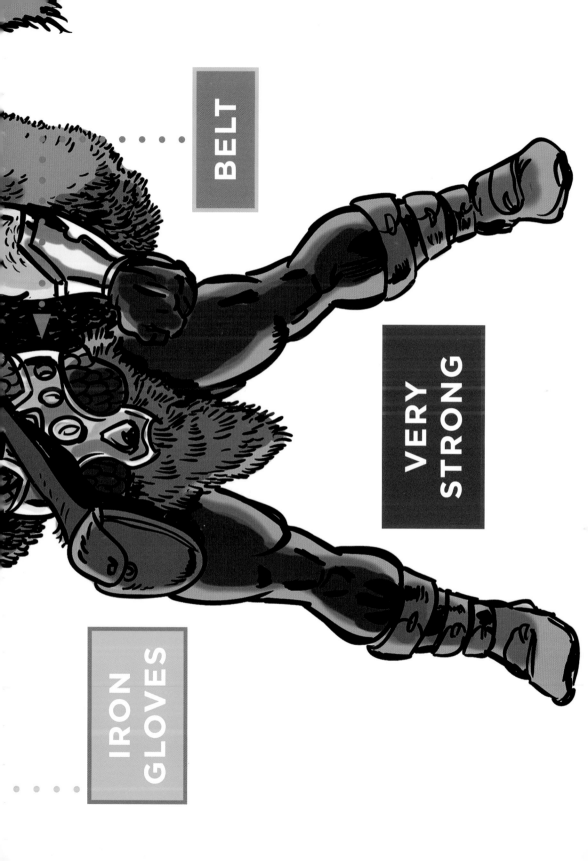

BELT

VERY STRONG

IRON GLOVES

Family

Stories say Thor's wife was Sif. Sif had long golden hair. It reminded people of wheat blowing in the breeze. She was the goddess of grain. Thor and Sif had a daughter, Thrud. They also had a son, Modi.

Not all Norse myths agree with each other. Some stories say Sif only had a daughter.

CHAPTER 4

The Final

Norse myths say the gods and giants will have a final battle. Thor will fight bravely. Stories say he will fight an **enormous** snake. Thor will **defeat** the snake, but its **venom** will kill him. The earth will burn and sink into the sea. Nearly all living things will die. Later, the earth will rise up again. New life will begin.

Many of the Norse stories were spoken. But hundreds of years ago, people found ancient poems. They told some Norse myths. That is how people know about Thor today.

Thor Today

People no longer believe the Norse gods exist. But some still think of Thor when they hear thunder. Thor has been a character in many TV shows, movies, and books. He is also a popular comic book superhero. His story is old. But it is still exciting today.

ancient (AYN-shunt)—from a time long ago

chariot (CHAR-ee-uht)—a carriage with two wheels that was raced and used in battle in ancient times

charm (CHAHRM)—a small object that is worn on a chain or bracelet

defeat (dih-FEET)—to win a victory over

duel (DOO-uhl)—a fight between two people

enormous (ih-NAWR-muhs)—very great in size or amount

myth (MITH)—a story told to explain a practice, belief, or natural occurrence

universe (YOO-nuh-vurs)—all of space and everything in it

venom (VEH-num)—a poison made by animals used to kill or injure

BOOKS

Napoli, Donna Jo. *Treasury of Norse Mythology: Stories of Intrigue, Trickery, Love, and Revenge.* Washington, D.C.: National Geographic, 2015.

Shecter, Vicky Alvear. *Thor Speaks!: A Guide to the Viking Realms by the Nordic God of Thunder.* Secrets of the Ancient Gods. Honesdale, PA: Boyds Mills Press, 2015.

Thompson, Ben. *Guts & Glory: The Vikings.* New York: Little, Brown and Company, 2015.

WEBSITES

Middle Ages: Vikings
www.ducksters.com/history/middle_ages_vikings.php

Ten Facts about the Vikings
www.ngkids.co.uk/history/10-facts-about-the-vikings

Vikings: Beliefs and Stories
www.bbc.co.uk/schools/primaryhistory/vikings/beliefs_and_stories/

INDEX

A

ancient Norse, 8, 9,
10–11, 12, 13, 15,
16–17, 18, 28

appearance, 4, 21,
22–23

C

chariot, 4, 7, 18

F

family, 12, 15, 25

H

hammer, 4, 7, 10–11, 18,
21, 22